The Berenstain Bears' Stories to Share

Stan & Jan Berenstain

Random House  New York

Visit us on the Web!
randomhouse.com/kids
BerenstainBears.com

Educators and librarians, for a variety of teaching tools, visit us at
randomhouse.com/teachers

ISBN: 978-0-307-93182-5
Library of Congress Control Number: 2011934350

Printed in the United States of America   10 9 8 7 6 5 4 3 2 1   First Edition

Contents

**The Berenstain Bears
and the Trouble with Friends**
5

**The Berenstain Bears:
No Girls Allowed**
35

**The Berenstain Bears
Go Out for the Team**
65

The Berenstain Bears and the TROUBLE WITH FRIENDS

When making friends,
the cub who's wise
is the cub who learns
to compromise.

Sister and Brother Bear, who lived with their mama and papa in the big tree house down a sunny dirt road deep in Bear Country, were not only sister and brother, they were playmates and they got along pretty well—most of the time.

But Brother was quite a lot older than Sister—almost two years—and sometimes he wasn't much interested in the games she wanted to play. Especially when Sister got a little bossy—which she sometimes did.

"Now," she said one day as she came out of the tree house with a big armload of her dolls and stuffed animals, "we're going to play tea party. You sit there and be the papa and I'll sit here and be the mama."

"Aw, gee, Sis," said Brother. "I'm too old to play tea party. Why, if Cousin Freddy or any of the guys saw me I'd never hear the end of it. Why don't you find somebody your own age to play tea party with?

"Besides, I have a date to go skateboarding with Freddy." And off he zoomed, leaving Sister all by her lonesome.

"All right for you!" she shouted.

"Oh, dear," said Mama, who was watching from the tree house window. "There goes Brother off to play with Freddy again. I do wish Sister had somebody her own age to play with."

"What about her school friends?" asked Papa, joining her at the window.

"They all live too far away," sighed Mama as she watched lonesome Sister pick up her trusty jump rope and start jumping with a friendly frog. Soon a butterfly joined in.

"She has her forest friends, the frogs and butterflies, to play with," said Papa.

"Frogs and butterflies are all very well," said Mama. "But they're not the same as having a cub friend your own age."

That's when Mama saw the moving truck out of the corner of her eye.

"Look!" she said. "A new family moving into the empty tree house down the road! It certainly would be nice if they had a cub Sister's age."

Sister saw the truck too—and the car following it.

"Somebody moving into the empty tree house!" she said. "I wonder if they have any cubs." And off she skipped down the road to investigate.

The truck stopped at the empty house and the moving bears began to unload it. The car pulled in behind the truck and the new family got out. There was a mama, a papa, and a little girl cub just about Sister's age!

Sister could hardly believe her good luck! Just what she needed—a little girl cub to jump rope, play tea party and house and school, and have all kinds of cub fun with! She could hardly wait to say hello. She skipped over and introduced herself.

"Hi! I'm Sister Bear. I'm six years old and I live just down the road."

"Hi!" said the new cub. "I'm Lizzy Bruin and this is my papa and mama, Mr. and Mrs. Bruin. I'm six years old too. May I try your jump rope? I can do Red Hot Pepper!"

And could she ever! Lizzy Bruin was the fastest rope jumper Sister had ever seen.

"I can jump to a thousand," said Sister.

"I can do a thousand and one," said Lizzy, returning the rope.

"A thousand and two," snapped Sister.

"A thousand and three," said Lizzy.

"Well, we'll just see about that! Let's have a jump-off here and now!" said Sister.

"Let's not and say we did!" said Lizzy. "Say! Isn't that a playground over there? Last one there is a rotten egg!" And off she ran with Sis doing her best to catch up.

"Well," said Mama, who had been watching from the window, "the new cub certainly is a lively little thing. She may be just what Sister needs."

Sister and Lizzy had quite an afternoon. They climbed to the top of the junglegym . . .

rode the seesaw . . .

and pushed each
other on the swings.

They played tag . . .

laughed and giggled . . .

rolled down a grassy bank . . .

and picked wild flowers for
their mamas.

"Why, thank you, Sister. How lovely!" said Mama, putting her wild flowers in water. "Well, what's your new friend like?"

"Her name is Lizzy, she's six years old, she's an only cub—and," Sister said, "she's a little bossy."

"Oh," said Mama. "Well, you certainly seemed to be having fun."

"Oh, yes!" said Sister. "I had a lot of fun! A little bossy—*and* a little braggy."

The next morning, bright
and early, the phone rang. It
was Sister's new friend, Lizzy.

21

"Want to come over and play school?" asked Lizzy.

"Okay," said Sister.

"Bring some of your dolls and stuffed animals," added Lizzy, "because mine aren't unpacked yet."

So Sister gathered up some of her favorite dolls and stuffed animals and headed for the tree house down the road.

"Come on in here," called Lizzy from the garage. "My mama and papa are still 'fixing up' and 'putting away,' so we're going to play in here. Who did you bring?"

"My best doll and stuffed animals," said Sister. "And this is my special teddy that I've slept with every night since I was a baby."

Lizzy had set up the garage like a schoolroom. There were boxes for the pupils to sit on, and there was another box for the teacher's desk. There was even a blackboard and chalk for lessons.

"This is going to be fun," thought Sister Bear as she began sitting her toys on the boxes. That's when she heard the tapping sound. It was Lizzy tapping on the desk. She had a pretend pointer in one hand and a piece of chalk in the other.

"Please be seated, Sister. It's time for your lessons. Today I'm going to teach you the alphabet. The first letter of the alphabet is—"

"Now, just a minute!" protested Sister. "Who said you were going to be teacher? When I play school *I'm* the teacher! And not only that—I already know my ABC's!"

"Sister Bear, if you don't sit down this minute, I'm going to keep you after school!" said Lizzy.

"Is that so?" shouted Sister. "Well, if you don't give me that pointer, I'm going to keep *you* after school!"

That's when Sister grabbed the pointer. Soon they were rolling around on the floor wrestling for the pointer, which broke in two.

"Now look what you did!" shouted Lizzy. "You broke my best pointer!"

"I'm not going to play with you ever again!" shouted Sister, gathering up her toys. "I'm going to take my dolls and go home!"

"Sister's mad and I'm glad!" shouted Lizzy as Sister marched out of the garage.

"Lizzy Lizzy in a tizzy!" Sister shouted back.

"Back so soon?" asked Mama when Sister returned looking like a storm cloud.

"I'm never going to play with that Lizzy Bruin again!" shouted Sister. "She's much too braggy and bossy! I don't need her to play school or anything else! It's much better playing by yourself! When you play by yourself you can do what you want when you want without having to worry about that Lizzy Bruin!"

"That's true," said Mama in a quiet voice. "Of course, there are some things you really can't do very well by yourself."

"Like what?" asked Sister.

"You'd have a pretty hard time pushing yourself on a swing," said Mama. "And I'd like to see you ride a seesaw by yourself. Most games like hopscotch and jacks take at least two to play. And it certainly is nice to have someone to laugh and giggle with."

"Maybe so," said Sister, "but Lizzy is much too braggy and bossy. Why does she have to be the teacher when we play school?"

"It seems to me," said Mama, taking Sister on her lap, "that Lizzy isn't the only cub that's braggy and bossy sometimes—and, of course, there is one thing you can do much better by yourself."

"What's that, Mama?"

"Be lonesome," said Mama quietly.

And that's when somebody knocked on the door.

It was Lizzy and she was carrying Sister's teddy.

"When Sister took all her dolls and went home, she forgot her teddy," she said. "And, well, I knew it was her special favorite that she slept with since she was a baby and I thought she might miss it."

"Why, thank you, Lizzy," said Mama. "That was very thoughtful of you."

"Thank you very much," said Sister, hugging her teddy.

"And you can be teacher if you want to," said Lizzy.

"Or," said Sister, "we can take turns being teacher."

"Terrific!" said Lizzy.

"Great!" said Sister, gathering up her doll and stuffed animals again. "Last one back to your garage is a rotten egg!"

33

And off she scooted,
laughing and giggling,
with Lizzy scampering
after her.

The Berenstain Bears

NO GIRLS ALLOWED

Is it so important that
He and she bears aren't the same
When what really matters is
How we play the game?

Ever since Sister Bear had been a tiny cub, she liked to tag along and play with Brother Bear and his friends. It was a bit of a nuisance because she slowed down their running . . .

"Wait for me!"

interfered with their climbing . . .

"Not so high!"

and messed up their marble games.

"Oh! That slipped!"

37

But as she grew older, things changed. She still liked to tag along with her older brother and his friends and it was no longer a *bit* of a nuisance: it was a BIG nuisance. She got to be a fast runner and outran Brother and his friends.

"Look at her go!" said Papa.

She got to be a good climber and outclimbed them.

"Oh, dear," said Mama. "I do wish she'd be more careful."

And she won all their marbles.

"Goodness! I hope they're not playing for keeps!" said Mama.

"It certainly is good to see Sister and Brother and their friends playing so nicely together," said Papa. "Look, they're organizing a baseball game."

"Yes," said Mama. "But it does worry me just a little that Sister is the only girl in the group."

"Now, Mama," said Papa. "It's not whether you're a he or a she that counts, it's how you play the game—look, she just hit a home run!"

"I agree," said Mama. "But think back—how would you have liked it when you were a cub if some little girl could outrun, outclimb, and outhit you?"

Papa thought for a moment.

"I wouldn't have liked it," he said.

42

Brother and his friends didn't like losing either. And what made it worse was the way Sister celebrated every time she won.

Her victory dance and cartwheels were annoying, but it was the war whoops that really got on everybody's nerves.

Then one day, when Sister was planning to tag along as usual, her playmates were nowhere to be seen.

No matter, she thought, and went about her business. She picked wild flowers for Mama and jumped rope with some butterflies.

When there were no cubs around the next day, she was puzzled.

But there was plenty to do—she had a tea party for her dolls and read some books.

45

But on the *third* day she began to wonder what was going on. "Where *are* those cubs?" she said aloud.

They weren't in the old climbing tree. They weren't playing marbles.

46

And they certainly weren't on the baseball field.

As she stood on the deserted field wondering where everybody was, she heard voices. They sounded like cubs' voices, and they were coming from the thicket.

She followed the sound into the thicket. What *were* those cubs up to? When she reached the edge of Frog Pond she found out!

What they were up to was building a secret clubhouse on Berrybush Island in the middle of Frog Pond! It had peepholes, watchtowers, and a little bridge—it was almost like a castle. What a wonderful surprise!

"Hi, gang!" she shouted.

She was so excited that she did her celebration dance, complete with cartwheels and war whoops! But Brother and the other boys didn't answer Sister's happy cry. Instead they ducked inside, then reached out and put the finishing touch on their new clubhouse: a sign that said "Bear Country Boys Club—NO GIRLS ALLOWED"!

As Sister stood there trying to think what to do next, there was a creaking sound. The bridge was a *drawbridge* and they were cranking it up! She was heartbroken.

"It isn't fair!" she wailed as she ran home from the thicket.

Bear Country Boy
NO GIRLS
ALLOWED

"You're absolutely right!" roared Papa.
"It *isn't* fair! Come, we're going back
there and *make* them take you into their
silly club—and if they don't, I'm going to
tear that clubhouse limb from limb!"

But Mama stopped them. "I don't think that's the answer," she said. "Those boys *are* being very unfair. Sometimes boys act that way— so do girls—but whoever does it is wrong. The important thing is not whether you are a boy or a girl, but the sort of person you are. . . .

"And, be that as it may, you can't *make* cubs want to play with you."

"No," said Sister, "but you can tear them limb from limb! Come on, Papa!"

"Wouldn't it be a better idea," suggested Mama, "for you to form your own club and build a secret clubhouse of your own?"

"Could I?" said Sister.

"This old climbing tree might be a good spot for it," said Papa. "And I'll help!"

"Terrific!" said Sister. "The first thing we'll need is a big sign that says 'NO BOYS ALLOWED'!"

"No," said Mama. "The first thing you need for a club is members."

That part turned out to be easy.
News of the No Girls Allowed club
traveled fast, and there were quite
a few other sisters who didn't like the
idea of being left out. They had a lot of
good ideas. Lizzie made a rope ladder that
they could wind up when they didn't want
visitors. Ellen brought a spyglass for
keeping watch. And Marsha had
the best idea of all—a tin-can
phone system.

With Papa Bear's help they
built a very fine clubhouse
high up in the old climbing
tree.

"Now for that sign!" said Sister. "Those boys were just being mean because I outhit them and won all their marbles! They're bad losers!"

59

"I suppose that's true," agreed Mama.
"But you know, there's such a thing as a
bad winner, too—someone who makes a
big braggy show every time she wins."
Sister Bear knew exactly who Mama was talking about.

"But it still isn't fair," Sister said.
"Well," said Mama, "I think we can work things
out. But first we have to celebrate the opening of
this very special clubhouse with some very special
refreshments: barbecued honeycomb and salmon!"
Now, if there's anything cubs are crazy about, it's
barbecued honeycomb and salmon—girl cubs . . .
and boy cubs. So Papa loaded up the barbecue.

The yummy smells reached into the thicket and floated right under the noses of the members of the Bear Country Boys Club . . .

. . . who followed their noses back to where the members of the Bear Country Girls Club were just pulling up their rope ladder.

"Something sure smells good," said Brother, speaking into the phone. The girls took a vote and decided to invite the boys up for honeycomb and salmon.

"How would you like to come back to our place for dessert?" said Brother. "Our berry crop is ripe for picking."

"Love to!" said Sister, and while the
whole gang headed for Frog Pond, Brother ran
ahead and quickly changed the clubhouse sign to say
"Bear Country Boys Club—GIRLS WELCOME"!
The berries were delicious.

The Berenstain Bears
GO OUT FOR THE TEAM

CHAMP

When little bears first
Show a will to compete,
It's hard for parents not to
Jump in with both feet.

Brother and Sister Bear, who lived with their mama and papa in the big tree house down a sunny dirt road deep in Bear Country, enjoyed the changing seasons— and the sports that went with them:

—football and soccer in the fall . . .

—basketball and
ice hockey in the
winter . . .

—and their favorite,
baseball in the spring.

As soon as Brother and Sister felt the first warmth of the spring sun, they got out their trusty ball, bat, and gloves and began limbering up for the season.

They played pitch-and-catch . . .

and practiced batting.

Why, they even studied up on the rules of the game.

Pretty soon some of their friends came to join in the baseball fun.

After a while Brother looked around and said, "Hey, I think we have enough for a game. Let's go over to Farmer Ben's back meadow and choose up sides."

Farmer Ben was a good neighbor. He had been allowing cubs to play baseball in his meadow for years. Of course, the grassy meadow wasn't a real baseball field, so there were a few problems and some special ground rules.

There were no foul lines, just base paths worn by year after year of cubs running the bases. So there were a lot of arguments about foul balls. There was a rule against sliding into second base, because second base was a rock. And any ball that was hit into the duck pond in left field was a ground-rule double and an automatic time-out while they fished it out.

But arguments, rocks, and duck ponds didn't worry Brother, Sister, and their friends. They chose up sides and started a game.

Sister had done some growing since last season, and when she went to bat she whacked her very first ground-rule double. All the cubs—and even the ducks—were surprised.

And her knowledge of the rules
came in handy when Cousin Freddie
forgot to touch second base on his
way to third. She called for the ball,
tagged second, and declared him out.
He made a big fuss, but she pointed out
that those were the rules.

"Isn't that right?" she asked Farmer Ben,
who was watching from the sideline.

"Right as rain," said Farmer Ben.

The game moved right along until
Brother hit a ball all the way into
the next field and Farmer Ben's goat
got it.

"Back so soon?" asked Papa, looking up from his paper as Brother and Sister trooped back home.

"Yep!" said Sister, holding up the ball. "Game called off on account of Farmer Ben's goat chewing the cover off the ball."

Papa was pretty impressed when he heard about Brother's hit and Sister's ground-rule double.

"Seems to me," said Papa, "that you cubs might want to think about playing some real baseball on a real baseball field. It says right here in the paper that the Bear Country Cub League is going to be holding tryouts pretty soon. You might want to sign up."

"Now, hold on," interrupted Mama. "That's a high-powered league over there, and those tryouts involve quite a lot of pressure."

"Pressure?" asked Sister. "What do you mean?"

"You'll be competing against lots of other cubs and not everybody is going to make the team," said Mama. "But you both play pretty well," she added, "so it's up to you."

"Won't hurt to drive over and have a look," said Papa.

"Wow!" said Brother when he saw the Cub League field. It was a real field with fences and foul lines and real bases and grandstands and everything.

And the teams wore uniforms! Brother and Sister signed up right then and there!

BEAR COUNTRY CUB LEAGUE

LAST YEAR'S CHAMPS

SIGN UP HERE

They got ready for the tryouts by practicing. They practiced fielding and hitting. Mama showed them how to choke up on the bat against fast pitching. They even practiced bunting and base running. But as tryout day drew near, they began to get a little nervous.

"Try to calm down," said Mama. "It's only a game. Besides, the worst that can happen is that you won't make the team. You can always try out again next year."

"No, that's not the worst that can happen," said Brother, looking gloomy. "The worst that can happen is if Sis makes the team and *I don't*!"

"I consider that a sexist remark!" snapped Sister angrily.

"Well, not completely," said Mama. "After all, Brother's older than you and he's very proud of his baseball ability."

"I see what you mean about pressure," said Sister.

Finally the day of the tryouts came. There were cubs all over the field—and league officials with clipboards and sunglasses so you couldn't see what they were thinking. Each cub had a number, and the officials moved around the field watching the cubs and making checks on their clipboards. Talk about pressure!

Brother and Sister were nervous at first. Sister missed an easy ground ball and Brother swung too hard at bat, missed the ball completely, and fell down on the seat of his pants. But as the tryouts continued, they both settled down and did a little better.

Brother remembered to choke up on the bat. He hit a good single and went to second base when the fielder bobbled the ball. Sister fielded some grounders well, and once when she was batting, the catcher dropped the third strike and she ran to first base even though she had struck out. There was a big fuss, but an official was watching and said she was right.

"Well, how did you do?" asked Mama when she and Papa came to pick the cubs up after the tryouts.

"Hard to say," answered Brother. "We certainly weren't the best."

"But we weren't the worst, either," said Sister. "Anyway—it's only a game and the worst that can happen is that we won't make the team."

"Yeah," sighed Brother. "We can always try again next year if we want to."

"When will you know?" asked Papa as they headed home.

"They're going to post the results on the bulletin board tomorrow," said Brother.

"Well," said Papa the next
day, "don't you think we ought
to drive over and check up?"
"I guess so," said Brother.
"May as well," said Sister.

When they reached the
field, Brother and Sister
ran to the bulletin board.

"Talk about pressure," said Papa, mopping
his brow as he and Mama waited in the car.
"Indeed," said Mama, fanning herself.

At last Mama and Papa heard a
shout as Brother and Sister burst out of
the crowd around the bulletin board.

"We made it! We made it!" they shouted, jumping for joy.

"There are four teams in the league!" shouted Sister. "The Cardinals, the Bluejays, the Oriolcs, and the Catbirds! We both made the Cardinals!"

"Terrific!" said Papa.

"Congratulations!" said Mama.

On the day of the first game, the cubs looked elegant in their uniforms, and Mama and Papa sat up front in the grandstand. Brother was up to bat against the Bluejays. The pitcher wound up and threw a fast ball. Brother watched it go by.

"Strike one!" called the umpire.

"That was no strike!" screamed Mama, waving her hat. "It was wide by a mile! Call yourself an umpire!"

"Mama, please!" hissed Sister from the sideline. "Calm down! And remember—it's only a game!"

"Sorry about that," said Mama. Then
she straightened her hat, sat down, and
enjoyed the rest of the game.

All About the Berenstains

Many years ago, when their two sons were beginning to read, Stan and Jan Berenstain created the endearing bear clan that shares their own family name.

Since the first book appeared in the 1960s, they have written and illustrated more than three hundred Berenstain Bears books in a dozen formats, but the most enduring are the stories in the groundbreaking First Time Books® series. These humorous, warmhearted tales of a growing family (the books started with one cub and ended up with three) deal with issues common to all families with children: sibling rivalry, friendship, school, visits to the doctor and dentist, holiday celebrations, time spent together and apart, competition, good manners, and many more.

Each First Time Book® presents a problem that's resolved—usually by Mama and Papa, but sometimes by Brother and Sister—with good sense and, above all, a sense of humor. Lessons are learned and values explained and passed to the next generation, always through the telling of a good story. The Berenstain Bears First Time Books® have sold millions of copies, a testament to their enduring appeal, to the fact that families everywhere can see themselves in the Berenstain Bears—and to the truth that a well-told tale is indeed timeless.